NORA'S ROOM

ENTR IF YOU DARE!

By
Jessica Harper

Illustrated by
Lindsay Harper duPont

HARPERCOLLINSPUBLISHERS

Nora's Room
Text copyright © 2001 by Jessica Harper
Illustrations copyright © 2001 by Lindsay Harper duPont
Printed in the United States of America.
All rights reserved.
www.harperchildrens.com

Library of Congress Cataloging-in-Publication Data
Harper, Jessica.
Nora's room / by Jessica Harper ; illustrated by Lindsay
Harper duPont.
p.   cm.
Summary: There's such a racket coming from Nora's room
that her mother imagines a series of outlandish events going
on up there.
ISBN 0-06-029136-2 — ISBN 0-06-029137-0 (lib. bdg.)
[1. Noise—Fiction.   2. Stories in rhyme.]   I. duPont,
Lindsay Harper, ill.   II. Title.
PZ8.3.H219 No   2001   00-32039
[E]—dc21   CIP
AC

1 2 3 4 5 6 7 8 9 10
❖
First Edition

To our parents, Paul and Cooie,
and our sister and three brothers
with a hey nonny nonny and a
Crash Bang Boom!

Sounds like a bear is dancing with a moose.
(They like to dance when they're on the loose.)

Sounds like hippos at a hippo hop.

Or when you pick up a piano
and you let it drop.

Like 16 pumpkins *falling* off a truck . . .

Or a couple of gorillas playing
duck, duck, duck . . .

Like London Bridge is REALLY falling down!

Or a couple of GIANTS . . . are sitting on a town!

Or a bunch of rhinos playing musical chairs!

CRASH! BANG! CRASH BANG BOOM!
Something's going on in Nora's room!

And the sign on her door says,
"Enter if you dare!"
So I say, "What's going on in there?"

And she says . . .

"Oh, nothing."